John Dilworth

The Pictorial Model of the Tabernacle

SALZWASSER
VERLAG

John Dilworth

The Pictorial Model of the Tabernacle

Reprint of the original, first published in 1859.

1st Edition 2022 | ISBN: 978-3-37513-344-3

Verlag (Publisher): Salzwasser Verlag GmbH, Zeilweg 44, 60439 Frankfurt, Deutschland
Vertretungsberechtigt (Authorized to represent): E. Roepke, Zeilweg 44, 60439 Frankfurt, Deutschland
Druck (Print): Books on Demand GmbH, In de Tarpen 42, 22848 Norderstedt, Deutschland

DILWORTH'S

PICTORIAL MODEL

OF

THE TABERNACLE.

THE PICTORIAL MODEL OF THE TABERNACLE:

Its Rites and Ceremonies,

AS INAUGURATED BY MOSES, AND PRACTISED UNDER HIS SUPERINTENDENCE.

WITH EXPLANATORY OBSERVATIONS,

BY

JOHN DILWORTH.

"Moses wrote of ME."—*John* v. 46.

ILLUSTRATIONS BY W. A. NICHOLLS.

LONDON:

G. J. STEVENSON, 54, PATERNOSTER ROW;

SUNDAY-SCHOOL UNION, 56, OLD BAILEY;

MANCHESTER: W. BREMNER, 11, MARKET STREET.

1859.

THE MOST HOLY PLACE.

INTRODUCTORY NOTICE.

THE following pages contain a pictorial model and explanation of the Tabernacle in the Wilderness, and at the same time illustrate a perfect model constructed under the author's inspection, the idea of which originated in a desire to render divine truth clear to the understanding of a Sunday-school class. Their teacher (the author) was led by this motive to the perusal of Kitto's "Pictorial Bible," and to the diligent study of the Book of Exodus, wherein are found the most minute instructions for the erection and arrangement of the Tabernacle. The frequent recurrence, in the sacred text, of the symbols of atonement, raised his interest in the subject to an intense degree, and he felt that to prepare a series of lessons for his class respecting it, would prove the best incentive to successful study.

With the valuable aid of enlarged copies of illustrations, by Kitto and Bagster, but more especially the former, he commenced an explanation of the Tabernacle, with its rites, to a Sunday-school class of young men. But, as he proceeded, he became convinced that a perfect comprehension of it would not be attained, until a complete model of it was constructed; and he resolved, if ever placed in circumstances to justify the expense, a model should be made. The goodness of God has at length permitted this ardent desire of his soul to be accomplished, and the model* with it explanations, he now dedicates, with devout

---

* This model is in the course of being exhibited gratuitously throughout the kingdom; and this work, whilst intended to form an independent medium of useful instruction, furnishes a lecture which may be delivered during the exhibition. The model was constructed by Mr. George Hollingshed, Carver and Gilder, late of Manchester, now of 4, Burton Street, Burton Crescent, London. It was executed under the superintendence of the owner, who has much pleasure in directing attention to the skill, care, and beautiful workmanship its constructor has displayed in its production.

gratitude, to Him, and to the use of "the Church which He hath purchased with His own blood," fervently trusting that they may prove valuable aids to teachers and parents, in conveying to children a clearer understanding of the relation in which Christ stands to them as their atoning Saviour. He hopes that even ministers of the Gospel may find them useful in conveying the elementary instruction, which is necessary to advanced spiritual knowledge.

In the execution of his undertaking, he has represented the Levitical Institutions, not according to the corruptions of later years, but as they were inaugurated by Moses, and practised under his superintendence. The more carefully the model and these explanations are compared with the sacred text, the more thorough will be the conviction that they manifest no errors of importance.

It is to be feared, that many persons look upon the Old Testament merely as a History of the Jewish Nation, without seeing in that people, and in the rites and ceremonies of their worship, the types of things to come. If directing attention to the subject lead any such to perceive the intimate connection between the Old and New Testaments, and how fully those types have been fulfilled in the blessed Redeemer, more especially if it lead them to put their trust in Him as their Saviour; the author will obtain the reward of his best hopes, and feel thankful to God for using him as an instrument in bringing about so happy a result.

CONTENTS.

LIST OF PICTURES.

THE
TABERNACLE IN THE WILDERNESS.

DIRECTIONS for making the Tabernacle form a part of the Old Testament Scriptures, concerning which the Apostle Paul says, "They are profitable for instruction in righteousness" (2 Tim. iii. 16). He says also, of the arrangements of the Tabernacle, detailed in the books of Exodus, Leviticus, Numbers and Deuteronomy, and represented here, that they are "patterns of things in the heavens" (Heb. ix. 23) ; "a shadow of heavenly things" (Heb. viii. 5) ; "a shadow of good things to come" (Heb. x. 1) ; and that we have the reality and substance of them in Christ and Christianity (Col. ii. 17 ; Gal. iii. 24 ; Rom. x. 4). Jesus Himself says, "Moses wrote of me". (John v. 46).

It becomes, then, the duty of the Church of Christ to study prayerfully, that they may form accurate conceptions of this shadow, and to compare it with the substance ; as each will be found to develop the meaning of the other.

Our beloved Saviour and His apostles were members of the great congregation of Israel, God's ancient Church ; and were practically conversant with the facts here represented. The figures of speech in which they convey the instructions of the New Testament, especially those most important to salvation, are chiefly supplied by the Tabernacle and its worship.

If this be so, are not these typical representations the very A B·C of New Testament knowledge ? Can a Christian be well instructed, who has not, as far as possible, made himself acquainted with them ?

Perhaps more need not be said, to secure a favourable consideration of the subject.

PREVIOUS HISTORY OF THE ISRAELITES.

Three thousand three hundred and fifty years ago, or 1491 B.C., the Israelites, after enduring cruel treatment as slaves in Egypt (Gen. xv. 13, 14), where they sojourned 430 years (Ex. xii. 40; i.; ii. 1—11*), were looked upon with pity by the God of their fathers (Ex. ii. 23—25; iii.), and permitted to depart ; their tyrannical masters being overawed by the plagues inflicted on them for their obstinate refusal to let them go. Jehovah, in a pillar of cloud, conducted them to the Red Sea, one of the boundaries of Egypt (Ex. xiv. 24; xiii. 21, 22; xiv. 1, 2). He made a path for them through the sea, piling up the waters in heaps, so that they formed a wall on each side (Psa. lxxviii. 13; Ex. xiv. 22), and commanded them to march across ; the pillar went from before their face and "stood behind" them, so as to be a cloud of darkness to the Egyptians, whilst it cast light upon the path of the advancing Israelites (Ex. xiv. 19, 20).

* The passages of Scripture are quoted in the order in which they are desired to be read.

The King of Egypt, with his troops, designing to drive them back and once more reduce them to slavery, pursued them even into the bed of the sea. Already the Israelites, followed by the cloud, had crossed in safety, when, in obedience to the will of God, expressed by Moses stretching forth his rod over the sea, the walls of water gave way, and covering Pharaoh and his host, their dead bodies strewed the coast of the peninsula of Sinai, into which their Almighty Captain had now introduced His rescued ones (Ex. xiv. 23—30).

These consisted of thirteen tribes, all the posterity of one man, called Israel, a name signifying Prince of God, and which Jehovah had given to Jacob (Gen. xxxii. 28). Each tribe bore the name of that son or grandson of Jacob from whom it descended.

Eleven of the men giving names to the tribes were sons of Israel, viz., Issachar, Judah, Zebulon, Simeon, Levi, Reuben, Gad, Asher, Dan, Napthali, Benjamin ; two were grandsons, by his son Joseph, viz., Ephraim and Manasseh (Gen. xlix. 1—27 ; xlviii. 1, 2).

The posterity of these thirteen men constituted the future kingdom of Israel (see the descendants of twelve of them mentioned as tribes in Numb. ii., and of the thirteenth, Numb. iii. 6). When the Scriptures speak of the tribes as twelve, Ephraim and Manasseh are counted only as one, being the joint representatives of their father, Joseph.

THE WILDERNESS.

Israel was now freed from bondage, and travelling in that region which intervened between Egypt and Canaan, the land promised to their great ancestors—to Abraham (Gen. xiii. 15 ; xv. 7, 18—21 ; xvii. 8), to Isaac (Gen. xxvi. 1—3), and to Israel, that is, Jacob (Gen. xxviii. 13, 14 ; xlviii. 3, 4), as the ultimate earthly home of their posterity.

To this land Jehovah had determined to conduct them. Before reaching it, however, he subjected them to much tribulation, chiefly arising out of their want of faith in Him, their Almighty Deliverer (Ex. xv., and to the end of Deuteronomy). They must have numbered at this time, men, women, and children, 2,500,000 —Dr. Kalisch, in his comment on Ex. xii. 37, says, *at least* 2,500,000 — a population equal to that of London and its suburbs. They had flocks and herds almost innumerable (Ex. xii. 37, 38).

The land they had left was a fruitful land, well watered, highly cultivated, and thickly peopled. The highest order of civilization the world knew prevailed there. Monuments of its arts and sciences continue to this day ; and they are so stupendous, that they draw visitors from all parts of the civilized world, and astonish them, even in this age of wonders.

Very different in character was the region into which the Israelites were now introduced. It was almost the reverse in every respect. Moses speaks of it as "a desert land and waste howling wilderness" (Deut. xxxii. 10) ; "a great and terrible wilderness, where there was no water" (Deut. viii. 15). And Jeremiah calls it "a land that no man passed through, and where no man dwelt" (Jer. ii. 6).

Its present condition verifies these descriptions. Burckhardt, Dr. Olin, Dr. Robinson, and other travellers, inform us, that its population, consisting of a few Arab tribes, does not number more than from 4,000 to 7,000 persons ; that there are scarcely any birds or other animals in it ; that it abounds in barren mountains, shifting sand-hills, and gravelly, flinty plains ; that it has little vegetation, the mountains being entirely devoid of it, what it has being chiefly scattered shrubs, food only for the camel; that the water is deficient in quantity, and generally bad in quality; and that the rain sometimes fails for two or three successive years.

Dr. Robinson, writing in April, 1838, after travelling in it seventeen days, says that " he had only once seen a blade of grass." He also adds, "We were told that many camels had died in the present year, owing chiefly to the excessive drought, there having been little rain (or according to the Arab mode of speech none) for now two seasons. As we saw the Peninsula, a body of 2,000,000 of men could not subsist a week in it without drawing supplies of water as well as provisions from a great distance."

Yet Jehovah supplied His rescued people in this dreadful desert, with every needful blessing, for a period of forty years! Of course He did so miraculously. "Man did eat angel's food." "He sent them meat to the full" (Psa. lxxviii. 25; Ex. xvi). And "He clave the rock in the wilderness, He gave them drink as out of the great depths." "He brought streams also out of the rock, and caused waters to run down like rivers" (Psa. lxxviii. 15, 16, 20; Numb. xx. 7—11; Deut. ix. 21; 1 Cor. x. 4). At the close of their pilgrimage, Moses says to the assembled nation, immediately before resigning his charge into the Divine hands, " I have led you forty years in the wilderness: your clothes are not waxen old upon you, and thy shoe is not waxen old upon thy foot" (Deut. xxix. 5).

THE CLOUD.

Their Divine Shepherd (Psa. lxxviii. 52) guided them through the desert *in* a pillar (Ex. xiii. 21). It was a cloud by day, and a fire giving light by night (Numb. ix. 15, 16; Deut. i. 29—33). He regulated the movements of the host from this pillar almost exclusively. Its standing still was a sign for them to halt, its moving forward to march (Numb. ix. 17—23; Ex. xl. 36—38). Towards Jehovah *in it* the people performed their outward acts of worship (Ex. xxxiii. 9, 10). *From it* He sometimes manifested satisfaction with their doings (Ex. xl. 34, 35; Lev. ix. 23, 24), sometimes displeasure (Lev. x. 2; Numb. xiv. 10; xvi. 35; xi. 1).

SINAI.

Slowly, by short stages, as they, their little ones, and their immense droves of cattle were able to bear, Jehovah, in this cloud, led them as an Eastern shepherd his flock, from the shores of the Red Sea, into that cluster of mountains called Horeb, and leaving them at the foot of one called Sinai, He made a throne of its granite head, its elevation above the level of the sea being 7,500 feet. " And it came to pass on the third day in the morning, that there were thunders and lightnings, and a thick cloud upon the mount, and the voice of the trumpet exceeding loud; so that all the people that was in the camp trembled. And Moses brought forth the people out of the camp to meet with God; and they stood at the nether part of the mount" (Ex. xix. 16, 17). On this occasion, He, in a voice which they that heard entreated to hear no more (Deut. iv. 12; Ex. xx. 19), proclaimed those Ten Commandments (Ex. xx. 1—17) which He afterwards, with His own "finger," engraved on stone (Ex. xxxi. 18; xxxiv. 1, 2, 28, 29).

Yielding to the desire of His people, God issued the rest of His laws through His usual medium, the mouth of His servant Moses the divinely appointed agent for inaugurating the institutions here represented (Deut. v. 22—31). These laws constituted the future political, civil, and ecclesiastical code of the nation, and they, as well as the Tables of the Covenant, were ordered to be deposited under the seat of His future throne (Deut. x. 5). He commanded a Tabernacle to be prepared, after a pattern shown to Moses in the Mount (Ex. xxv. 8, 9), that therein the symbol of His presence might be manifested, that He might dwell among the children of Israel, and be their God (Ex. xxix. 45). The instructions for the erection and arrangement of this Tabernacle and its furniture are very minute. By careful study of their dimensions and proportions, we have been able to present a model for the inspection of such as desire information on this interesting subject.

The Tabernacle was admirably suited for its purpose, and adapted to the circumstances of the people. They were journeying from Egypt to Canaan, and were destined to wander for a long period of time in the intermediate desert, as a sort of national training school. As we have seen, it was not fitted to supply them with many comforts. Their dwellings they had to carry with them—they were tents (Numb. xxiv. 5). The Tabernacle which their Heavenly King ordered to be made for Him was also a tent (Ex. xxv. 8, 9). *Tabernacle* means *tent*.

THE ENCAMPMENT.

When the Tabernacle was erected, it became, by the Divine command, the centre of a vast encampment, of probably 2,500,000 people, extending, according to Josephus, a circuit of twelve miles (Num. ii. iii. 14—38). This mighty encampment is represented on the opposite page, and it is believed, with considerable accuracy. The Tabernacle, with the pillar of cloud resting upon it, and spreading itself so as to shade the whole encampment from the heat of an almost tropical sun (Ps. cv. 39), is seen in the centre of the picture surrounded by its court (Ex. xl. 38 ; Numb. ix. 15—23).

Between it and the first line of tents, which were pitched "far off about the Tabernacle" (Numb. ii. 2), a reserved space is seen, on which the nation assembled before Jehovah for worship and instruction. A thin line of tents surrounds this reserved space; these are the tents of Levi. This tribe was commanded to dwell all round the Tabernacle, between the rest of the tribes and their God, to preserve them from His wrath (Numb. i. 53), by the exercise of that mediatorial work to which it was appointed. On the right or east side, this line consisted of the following tents: the tents of Moses; of Aaron, the high-priest of Israel; and of Aaron's four sons, the first common priests. These were the only Levitical tents permitted to be pitched at that side (Numb. iii. 38). Behind the Levitical line, are the tents of the other twelve tribes of Israel. They consist of twelve groups, with the standard of each tribe placed at its head, nearest the Levitical line. The three groups on the right, or east side, represent the tents of Issachar, Judah, and Zebulon (Numb. ii. 3—9). The three on the lower, or south side, were those of Simeon, Reuben, and Gad (Numb. ii. 10—16). The three on the left, or west side, those of Manasseh, Ephraim, and Benjamin (Numb. ii. 18—24). The three on the upper, or north side, those of Asher, Dan, and Napthali (Numb. ii. 25—31).

The appearance of this encampment is best described in the

No. 1.

language of the wicked prophet Balaam, who once beheld it from a commanding position:—

" From the top of the rocks I see Him" (doubtless referring to the Lord Jehovah in the pillar of the cloud upon the Tabernacle), "and from the hills I behold Him. Who can count the dust of Jacob, and the number of the fourth part of Israel? How goodly are thy tents, O Jacob, and thy tabernacles, O Israel! As the valleys are they spread forth, as gardens by the river's side, as the trees of lign aloes which the Lord hath planted, and as cedar trees beside the waters. God brought him forth out of Egypt; he hath as it were the strength of an unicorn: he shall eat up the nations his enemies, and shall break their bones. He couched, he lay down as a lion, and as a great lion: who shall stir him up? Blessed is he that blesseth thee, and cursed is he that curseth thee" (Numb. xxiii. 9, 10; xxiv. 5, 6, 8, 9).

THE TABERNACLE AND ITS COURT.

The Tabernacle was first erected in the Desert of Sinai, 1490 B.C. To enable us to realize the great antiquity of the Tabernacle and its institutions, we may observe, that about fifty years before Christ visited our world in the flesh to purchase man's salvation, Julius Cæsar landed on our shores, finding our forefathers naked, painted savages. About 1,400 years earlier than that, the Tabernacle, with the Glory of Israel resting upon it in the pillar of cloud, was presented to the admiring gaze of the " many thousands of Israel" encamped around it.

Its cost was defrayed chiefly by the voluntary contributions of the people, and probably amounted, including the dress of the priests, to not less than £250,000 (KITTO's *Pictorial Bible*); and yet the liberality of the people was such, that their gifts were much more than sufficient for the purpose, and Moses caused it to be proclaimed throughout the camp: "Let neither man nor woman make any more work for the offering of the sanctuary," and so "the people were restrained from bringing" (Ex. xxxvi. 5, 6). The value of the precious metals alone, which were used in the construction of this Tabernacle, must have been immense. The Sacred Record gives the weight of gold, silver, and brass used (Ex. xxxviii. 24—29), which Dr. Kitto says was worth £213,320 3s. 6d. of our money. The wood used in its construction was of a very enduring character; a proof of which lies in the fact, that this Tabernacle was the house around which the Israelites worshipped till David removed the Ark from Kirjath-jearim to a tent on Mount Zion, Jerusalem (1 Chron. xiii. 5—14, and xv. 1—28), and at which they assembled occasionally till Solomon erected the Temple (2 Chron. i. 3); a period of 487 years. Our version calls it " shittim wood." It is supposed to have been obtained from the Acacian family of plants. Dr. Kalisch invariably translates the the Hebrew word for this wood "Acacia wood."

The Divine Architect gave His measurements in cubits. The learned do not agree as to the precise English measure of the Hebrew cubit. On the authority of Kitto and others, we have adopted twenty-one inches. The Tabernacle Model, its furniture, and conciliatory offerings (at present being exhibited at the Sunday School Union, London), are constructed on a scale of one inch to twenty-one inches. To form a correct estimate of the size imagine them to be about twenty-one times as large.

The structure consisted of two chambers (Ex. xxvi. 33; Heb. ix. 1, 2, 3), and a court open to the heavens (Ex. xxvii. 9). The first chamber was called the "Holy Place" (Heb. ix. 2 ; Ex. xxvi. 33); the second, the "Most Holy" (Ex. xxvi. 33) ; the "Holiest of all" (Heb. ix. 3). This last received its title from the fact, that the cloud, in which Jehovah manifested His presence, rested therein on a throne (Lev. xvi. 2), evidently ascending through the roof as here represented.

THE COURT.

The court was bounded by sixty pillars (Ex. xxvii. 10—16). Their capitals were of silver, their shafts were brass, and they rested on sockets of brass (Ex. xxvii. 10, 11, 17, 18). They were made secure by cords, extended from the capitals to tent-pins made of brass, and driven into the ground on either side (Ex. xxvii, 19). They appear to have been further secured by silver rods connecting their capitals (see Dr. Kalisch's translation of Ex. xxvii. 17). From the capitals was suspended a linen curtain (Ex. xxvii. 9, 11, 12, 14, 15), probably of open network, so as to permit the tribes in the open space outside to witness the proceedings within; none but the officiating tribe being permitted to approach the dwelling of the Most High, nearer than the altar of the court. A curtain of needlework of superior quality, wrought in blue, purple, and scarlet threads, probably of wool (Dr. Kalisch), on a linen foundation, was suspended from four of the pillars in the centre of the east side, so as to form the door of entrance (Ex. xxvii. 16). In the picture of the Tabernacle and its Court (No. 3, page 17), Levites are seen holding up this curtain.

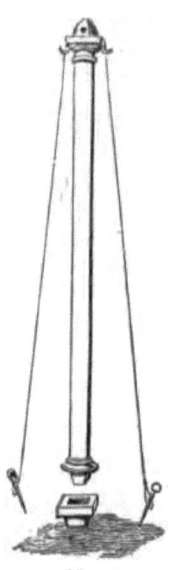

No. 2.

THE ALTAR OF BURNT-OFFERING.

In the Court was the Altar (Ex. xxvii. 1), called the "Altar of Burnt-offering" (Ex. xl. 10). On it were always burning portions of propitiatory animals, whose blood had been taken and offered to God as an atonement for sin. The fire was never suffered to go out (Lev. vi. 13). Its use is best given in the language of Scripture, "to make reconciliation upon" (Lev. viii. 15), that is, between God and His offending people.

Of like service was the Cross (Col. i. 20—22), which this Altar doubtless prefigured. On it, as the New Testament teaches, Christ made reconciliation with God for us.

The rite of reconciliation was performed by the Levitical priests, who, to this end, sprinkled upon the altar the blood of the reconciling animals, which the penitent brought for that purpose. So Christ, of whom these priests and sacrifices are but the figures, made peace with God for us by His own blood on the Cross.

The Altar was made of wood, covered with plates of brass, and having hooks, called "horns," at each corner, probably as an emblem of power. They were sometimes used for securing the reconciling victims previous to sacrificing them. The Psalmist says, "Bind the sacrifice with cords to the horns of the altar" (Ps. cxviii. 27). Its covering was a grating of brass (see pictures, pages 17 and 40), through which the ashes of the sacrifice passed into a chamber

No. 3.

below ; probably a door was placed on one side for their convenient removal. Two of its sides were provided with rings, through which wooden staves, overlaid with brass, were passed, to enable the Levites to carry it on their shoulders when the nation, headed by the symbol of Divine Majesty, was on its march. When the Altar was in use, these staves were withdrawn. Steps were forbidden (Ex. xx. 26); and as, from the height of the Altar, it is evident that the sacrifices could not conveniently be placed and arranged on it without an ascent of some kind, we have supposed that there was an embankment of earth forming an inclined plane on three sides, the fourth being occupied by the door. Lev. ix. 22 says that Aaron came *down* from offering the sin-offering and the burnt-offering and the peace-offerings. When Moses had consecrated Aaron to the office of high-priest of Israel, and Aaron had for the first time officiated at the Altar, by presenting sacrifices to the Lord on behalf of the assembled nation, " there came a fire out from before the Lord, and consumed upon the Altar the burnt-offering and the fat : which when all the people saw, they shouted, and fell on their faces" (Lev. ix. 24).

On this Altar, morning and evening, the high-priest burnt a lamb, having first offered its blood as an atonement for the national sin (Ex. xxix. 38—42). In the picture of the Tabernacle and its Court (page 17), Aaron, the high priest, is represented as so engaged. His four sons, the assistant common priests, are standing at the foot of the Altar ; and the twelve elders, representing the nation, form a semicircle behind them, bowing reverently.

The Lamb was required to be free from all bodily defects (Lev. xxii. 19-25). When brought to the Altar by the elders, the high priest figuratively transferred the transgressions of the nation to it, by placing his hands on its head. He then slew it, received its blood and offered it to God, for the people, by sprinkling it upon the Altar — the blood of the innocent as an atonement for the sins of the guilty. The whole animal was then consumed upon the Altar, and so the reconciliation was completed.

All this was figurative, and prophetical of Christ and His great atoning work, and throws much light on those passages of Holy Scripture which refer to them ; as, for example, "Behold the Lamb of God which taketh away the sin of the world" (John i. 29, 36) ; "Redeemed with the precious blood of Christ, as of a lamb without blemish and without spot" (1 Pet. i. 18, 19) ;

No. 4.

'Who His ownself bare our sins in His own body

on the tree" (1 Pet. ii. 24) ; " For Christ hath once suffered for sins the just for the unjust" (1 Pet. iii. 18) ; " Christ died for the ungodly " (Rom. v. 6) ; " He hath made Him to be sin for us, who knew no sin" (2 Cor. v. 21) ; " He was wounded for our transgressions, He was bruised for our iniquities : the chastisement of our peace was upon Him ; and with His stripes we are healed. He is brought as a lamb to the slaughter, and as a sheep before her shearers is dumb, so He openeth not His mouth. He was cut off out of the land of the living : for the transgression of my people was He stricken" (Isa. liii. compared with Acts viii. 32—35). " This is my blood of the new testament, which is shed for many for the remission of sins " (Matt. xxvi. 28).

Both the Old and New Testaments teach, that sin can be forgiven only by the shedding of blood as an atonement, and that without this there is no pardon.

THE LAVER.

A laver of brass also was placed in this court, between the altar and the Tabernacle (see picture 3, p. 17). Its use was to hold water wherewith the priests were to wash their hands and feet before entering the Tabernacle or officiating at the altar. The neglect of this duty was visited with the penalty of death (Ex. xxx. 20, 21).

No. 5.

This picture represents Aaron, the high-priest, receiving the required ablution at the hands of his son, one of the assistant common priests.

Doubtless the washing of the priests' hands suggested to David such forms of expressing his pious intentions as this—" I will wash mine hands in innocency ; so will I compass Thine altar, O Lord " (Ps. xxvi. 6).

The laver was made of the brazen mirrors which the women of Israel were in the habit of carrying with them to their worship at the Tabernacle, according to a custom they seem to have learned in Egypt. By thus appropriating the mirrors, Moses probably intended to condemn and put a stop to the practice (Ex. xxxviii. 8 ; 1 Peter iii. 3, 4).

THE TABERNACLE.

We now proceed to the description of the Tabernacle itself, a sketch of which is given without its coverings, that its construction may be seen. The divine record states that it was constructed with sockets, boards, pillars, veils, curtains, coverings.

No. 6.

THE COVERINGS.

It will be convenient to commence with the coverings—of these there were four. The outer one, our translation says, was made of badgers' skins (Ex. xxvi. 14). This rendering of the Hebrew word, however, is rejected by the learned. Our translators seem to have had difficulty in determining what animal's skin the Hebrew word represents. The best authorities are in favour of the seal, whose skin is frequently used for tent-covering.

The next covering is said to have been rams' skins dyed red. The next, called in the sacred text a curtain, was made of goats' hair. It was constructed of eleven parts ; six of these were so united as to form one curtain, and the remaining five another. When these two large curtains were brought together over the Tabernacle, they also were made to form one, by being fastened together with fifty taches (i.e. hooks or buttons) of brass (Exodus xxvi. 11).

The last, also called a curtain, was wrought with the needle on a linen foundation, with blue, purple, and scarlet threads, probably woollen (Dr. Kalisch). It had also representations of the cherubim wrought on it, probably with gold threads (Ex. xxvi. 1). This curtain consisted of ten parts. Five were united so as to form one curtain, and five another (Ex. xxvi. 3). When these two large curtains were drawn over the Tabernacle they also were made to form one, by being fastened together by fifty taches (i.e. hooks or buttons) of gold to loops of blue (Ex. xxvi. 4, 5).

The sacred record tells us that the wise-hearted women spun the goats' hair, blue, purple, scarlet, and linen thread (Ex. xxxv. 25, 26), and the wise-hearted men made the curtains (Ex. xxxvi. 8).

THE BOARDS.

Three sides of the Tabernacle were constructed with boards overlaid with gold—twenty of them formed the north side (Exodus xxvi. 20), twenty the south side (Ex. xxvi. 18), and eight the west end (Ex. xxvi. 22, 23). Each board rested on two heavy blocks of silver called sockets (Ex. xxvi. 19, 21, 25). The boards were dropped into them by means of two tenons, for the reception of which two corresponding holes in the sockets were prepared (Ex. xxvi. 17).

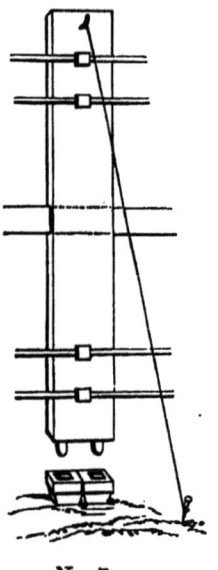

No. 7.

On each board there appears to have been four golden rings (Ex. xxvi. 29). The boards were bound together by wooden bars, overlaid with gold, and running through these rings from one end to the other (Ex. xxvi. 26—27), whilst another bar seems to have been shot through the boards themselves at their centre (Ex. xxvi. 28; xxxvi. 33.)

The west-end corners were fastened together by rings at their tops and bottoms (Ex. xxvi. 24). By this arrangement three walls were formed, as compact as can well be conceived.

The sides of the building were kept from falling in by cords which extended from the top of each board to tent-pins of brass outside, by which they were firmly pinned to the ground (Ex. xxxviii. 20). They were kept from falling outwards by the great weight of the coverings.

We have said the Tabernacle was divided into two chambers—the Holy Place and the Most Holy Place.

THE HOLY PLACE.

At the entrance of the Holy Place was a curtain, suspended by golden hooks from five wooden pillars, overlaid with gold (see picture 3 of the Tabernacle and its Court, p. 17). It resembled probably, in all respects, that at the entrance of the Court. These pillars rested on blocks of brass called sockets (Ex. xxvi. 36, 37).

Lifting up the veil, the priest entered the Holy Place, of which the picture opposite is a representation.

Here the high-priest and common priests officiated daily.

No. 8.

The "Candlestick."

The Holy Place contained a Candlestick. It was made of "pure gold," and was really a stand for lamps, richly ornamented with figures of the almond blossom. It had seven branches, was a talent in weight, and worth £5,475 of our money (Ex. xxv. 31—39). A lamp of olive oil was placed on each branch. In the picture No. 9, the high-priest is represented dressing these lamps, a duty he performed every morning (Ex. xxvii. 20, 21 ; xxx. 7, 8).

No. 9.

Table of Shewbread.

The Holy Place contained also a table, called the table of shew-bread. It was made of wood, overlaid with gold, and had a crown of gold around its top (Ex. xxv. 23—30 ; xxvi. 35).

During the marchings of the camp it was carried by the Levites, by means of wooden staves overlaid with gold passed through golden rings (see Pictures 10 and 8).

It was called the table of shewbread, because each tribe was re-presented on it in the dwelling of the Lord by a loaf of unleavened bread. The loaves lay upon it in two piles, on golden dishes each pile having a golden "pot" on its top, from which burning frank-incense was smoking (Lev. xxiv. 5—7).

Golden vessels, some containing salt (Lev. ii. 13) and others wine, were probably always upon this table (KITTO's *Pictorial Bible*). The loaves are described by the Lord as " the bread of their God "

C. P NICHOLLS

No. 10.

(Lev. xxi. 6, 8, 17, 21, 22). The loaves were changed every Sabbath day (Lev. xxiv. 8). The old ones were required to be eaten by the priests alone, and only in the Holy Place (Lev. xxiv. 9).

ALTAR OF INCENSE.

The last important article which the Holy Place contained, was an Altar on which to burn incense. It was made of wood, overlaid with gold. Its top was surrounded with a border of gold called a crown. Two wooden staves, overlaid with gold, and passed through golden rings, enabled the Levites to carry this altar when the nation was on its march (Ex. xxx. 1—6).

The high-priest of Israel commenced the morning and evening public worship by offering incense on this altar (Ex. xxx. 7, 8). In picture 8, he is represented performing this ceremony ; but in picture 11, p. 27, as explained in p. 35.

The time of offering incense was the hour of public prayer (Luke i. 10). Burning incense of sweet odour was an emblem of prayer. David used it as such. "Let my prayer be set forth before Thee as incense" (Ps. cxli. 2). The apostle John also (Rev. viii. 4 ; v. 8).

THE MOST HOLY PLACE.

Separating the Holy Place from the Holiest of all, were four pillars of wood overlaid with gold, and a vail suspended from them by golden hooks. This vail was a piece of needlework, wrought with blue, purple, and scarlet threads, probably of wool, on a foundation of linen. Representations of the cherubim were wrought upon it probably with gold threads (Ex. xxvi. 31, 32) ; see picture of Holy Place, p. 23 ; so that it resembled the roof-curtain (Ex. xxvi. 1). It was a similar vail, separating the Holy from the Most Holy Place in the Temple at Jerusalem, which by miraculously rending in two from top to bottom (Mat. xxvii. 50, 51), when our great High Priest Jesus (Heb. iii. 1) offered His blood on the cross to God, for the pardon of our sins (Heb. ix. 14; Mat. xxvi. 28), showed that thereby He had opened wide the gate of the true Holy of Holies to all believers

No. 11.

(Heb. x. 19). The apostle makes use of it as a figure of the body of Jesus, in that passage of sacred scripture, where he says :—"Having therefore, brethren, boldness to enter into the Holiest by the blood of Jesus, by a new and living way, which He hath consecrated for us, through the vail, that is to say, His flesh " (Heb. x. 19, 20).

The four pillars from which this vail was suspended rested on blocks of silver, called sockets (Ex. xxvi. 32). There were, in all, 165 of these sockets. The sixty underneath the pillars of the court were of brass (Ex. xxvii. 10—16). The five underneath the pillars at the entrance of the Holy Place were of brass (Ex. xxvi. 37). The four underneath the pillars at the entrance of the Most Holy Place were of silver (Ex. xxvi. 32). The ninety-six forming the foundation of the boards were of silver (Ex. xxvi. 19—21, 25).

Raising the vail the high-priest entered the Most Holy Place.

THE ARK.

All that the Most Holy Place contained was the throne of Jehovah, called the ark. The ark was a box of wood (*ark* means *box* or *chest*), overlaid within and without with "pure gold" (Ex. xxv. 10, 11). The top was ornamented with a border, called a crown of gold (Ex. xxv. 11).

No. 12.

Two wooden staves, overlaid with gold, and passed through golden rings, enabled the priests to carry this ark when the nation was on its march (Ex. xxv. 12—14).

The lid of the ark was the seat of the heavenly king. It was called the Mercy-seat (Ex. xxv. 17). It was of "pure gold," and standing on each end, "with wings stretched forth on high," and faces looking towards the mercy-seat, were golden representations of the cherubim (Ex. xxv. 19, 20 ; 1 Pet. i. 12).

When the camp was at rest, Jehovah, in the pillar of cloud, rested on this seat between the cherubim. When he commanded Moses to make the ark, He told him that He would meet with him and commune with him from above the mercy-seat, from between the cherubim, of all things which he would give in commandment to the children of Israel (Ex. xxv. 22).

It is to the Lord, considered as occupying this position, that the Psalmist says — "Thou that dwellest between the cherubim, shine forth" (Ps. lxxx. 1). The Lord reigneth; let the people tremble : He sitteth between the cherubim; let the earth be moved" (Ps. xcix. 1).

The ark contained two tables of stone, called the Tables of the Covenant, as having engraved upon them, with the "finger of God," the conditions of His engagement to friendly relations with His people as their king (Deut. ix. 9—17; x. 1—5).

It also contained a roll of the general laws of the kingdom, with its history down to the entrance into Canaan, probably as they were contained in the books of Genesis, Exodus, Leviticus, Numbers, and Deuteronomy (Deut. xxxi. 24, 26). This roll was probably made of sheep-skins, dyed red (KITTO's *Pictorial Bible*).

The ark also contained that rod of Aaron, the High Priest of Israel, wherewith Jehovah—by causing the dead stick to bear almond blossoms during the night, whilst the rods representing the other tribes, and put up with it in the holy place, remained dead—once for all convinced the rebellious nation, that the Lord would have none but the tribe of Levi in charge of His sanctuary, nor permit any but the Aaronites, who were members of it, to exercise the office of priest (Numb. xvi., xvii. ; read also Heb. ix. 4; v. 1—4).

The ark contained also a "golden pot" of that mysterious bread with which the Lord miraculously fed His people, during their forty years' pilgrimage (Ex. xvi. 32—35; Heb. ix. 4). Jesus refers to this bread as a type of Himself, saying, "The bread of God is He which cometh down from heaven, and giveth life unto the world." "I am that bread of life" (John vi. 31—35).

The symbol of Divine Majesty was the only light which the Holy of Holies contained (1 Kings viii. 12).

Human footsteps entered this Holy Place only once a year (Heb. ix. 7, 8). This was on the great day of atonement or reconciliation, when the sacred tent—too polluted by the past year's sins of the camp, in the midst of which it stood, to be any longer the abode of the "Holy Lord God of Hosts," without undergoing purification—was cleansed by the blood of atonement, and the people also were cleansed in an unusually solemn manner (Lev. xvi. 16).

On this occasion, the high priest appeared before the ark, with a vessel containing blood, taken from the propitiatory animals previously slain before the altar in the court. Having first placed a golden censer of smoking incense before the ark, he sprinkled a little of the blood with his finger upon Jehovah's mercy-seat, and seven times before the mercy-seat (Lev. xvi. 12—15). The figure of the high priest (picture 12, p. 28) represents him so engaged.

We have the authority of holy scripture for saying, that herein he resembled Jesus. "But Christ being come an high priest of good things to come, by a greater and more perfect tabernacle, not made with hands, that is to say, not of this building; neither by the blood of goats and calves, but by His own blood He entered in once into the holy place, having obtained eternal redemption for us." "For Christ is not entered into the holy places made with hands, which are the figures of the true; but into heaven itself, now to appear in the presence of God for us" (Heb. ix. 11, 12, 24).

When, by the ascent of the symbol of Jehovah from the mercy-seat, he commanded Israel to strike their tents and march, the sacred throne, with the other furniture of the tabernacle, was carefully covered by the high priest from profane gaze. Then the Levites lifted up the ark upon their shoulders, that it might take its place behind the cloud, and at the head of the moving host, and Moses, addressing the Lord in the cloud, said, "Rise up, Lord, and let Thine enemies be scattered; let them that hate Thee flee before Thee" (Numb. x. 35).

When the Lord, in the cloud, had "searched out a resting-place" for His people (Numb. x. 33), and rested upon it, the tribes pitched their tents in the prescribed order; the tabernacle was reared in their midst, and the throne and other furniture were arranged in their accustomed places. Then Moses again addressed the Divine Majesty in the pillar of cloud, and said, "Return, O Lord, unto the many thousands of Israel" (Numb. x. 36). Then, doubtless, the cloudy pillar was seen to rise and take its usual position, upon and within His tabernacle, between the golden cherubim of the mercy-seat.

THE "ORACLE."

The Scriptures frequently call the Most Holy Place the "Oracle" (1 Kings vi. 16). This was because from thence, after the erection of the Tabernacle, the Lord issued His oracles, i.e. commands, etc., to His people, and answers to their inquiries. The history of Israel supplies many instances (Numb. xxvii. 21; Judges i. 1, 2; xx. 18, 26—28; 1 Sam. xxii. 13).

It is said of Moses, who, as the divinely appointed agent in initiating the Levitical institutions, had frequently to go into the Holy Place, to learn the will of the Lord, that when he did so, "he heard the voice of one speaking unto him from off the mercy-seat, that was upon the ark of the testimony, from between the two cherubim" (Numb. vii. 89).

PRIESTS AND LEVITES.

The figure to the right, No. 14, page 31, is the High Priest of Israel; that to the left, the Common Priest. They represent the Levitical priesthood, whereby Christ was prefigured till He came, as the Intercessor with God for His people, the Maker and Preserver of peace between Him and men.

Its members were required to be free from "blemish," that is, without bodily imperfection. For example :—If a man of the priestly stock had "lost a finger," or had a "finger too many," had a "crooked back," or "flattened nose," he was incapacitated from exercising the priestly functions (Lev. xxi. 16—23). The Priests were permitted to marry, but the High Priest was not allowed to marry a woman of bad character, or even a widow; she must be a virgin Israelite (Lev. xxi. 13, 14).

Their Dress.—The sacred record does not state how the mere Levite was to be attired. The priests being types of Christ, their dress is described with great particularity. The dress of the common priests consisted of a pair of drawers (Ex. xxviii. 42), a figured white robe, girdle, and turban (Ex. xxviii. 40), probably of linen.

The dress of the high priest resembled that of the common priest so far (Ex. xxviii. 40—43). And, indeed, he performed some portions of his official work in this dress alone ; for example, the sprinkling of the blood on the mercy-seat, on the great day of atonement. But in all cases, when he had completed the principal part of his atoning work, he was robed as here represented (Lev. xvi. 23, 24).

No. 13.   No. 14.

The first robe was precisely the same as that of the common priest. The second was blue, and was a sleeveless coat, hanging from the shoulders only. Around its lower border was suspended a series of golden bells, separated from one another by pomegranates wrought in wool (Ex. xxviii. 31—35). The use of these bells is explained by the text, " And his sound shall be heard when he goeth in unto the Holy Place before the Lord, and when he cometh out, that he die not " (Ex. xxviii. 35). This blue coat was named, the Robe of the Ephod (Ex. xxviii. 31).

The Ephod was similar in form, wrought out of gold and blue, purple and scarlet threads, probably of wool, on a linen foundation

(Ex. xxviii. 6). It was fastened over each shoulder by a buckle, an onyx stone set in gold (Ex. xxviii. 7, 9—12). The names of the twelve tribes were engraved thereon ; six on one stone, and six on the other (Ex. xxviii. 9—11). Thus, ancient Israel, and its interests before Jehovah, were made to rest on the shoulders of the high priest.

In like manner, the Great High Priest, Jesus, bears on his shoulders the interests of modern Israel (Is. ix. 6) — the Church redeemed with His "precious" blood.

The Ephod was bound to the waist with a girdle of materials similar to the ephod (Ex. xxviii. 8).

A Breastplate was suspended from the shoulder-buckles of the ephod by golden chains, attached to rings of gold in its upper corners ; and to similar rings in the lower corners, laces of blue were attached to connect it with the girdle of the ephod (Ex. xxviii. 22—28).

The Breastplate was a piece of needlework, square when doubled, wrought on linen with gold and blue, purple, scarlet, probably woollen thread. It had settings of precious stones in four rows (Exodus xxviii. 15—17). The sacred text says that these stones were :—the sardius, the topaz, and the carbuncle (Ex. xxviii. 17), the emerald, the sapphire and the diamond (Ex. xxviii. 18), the ligure, the agate and the amethyst (Ex. xxviii. 19), the beryl, the onyx and the jasper (Ex. xxviii. 20). On the stones of the breastplate were engraven the names of the twelve tribes of Israel, one on each stone (Ex. xxviii. 21). The divine record describing the object of this, says, that so Aaron the high priest " shall bear the names of the children of Israel in the breast-plate of judgment upon his heart, when he goeth in unto the holy place, for a memorial before the Lord continually" (Ex. xxviii. 29). Thus does Jehovah's typical High Priest seem to have been taught that the affections of his heart should be set on His people Israel, to watch over their interests before Him. Is not this touchingly suggestive of the relation of Christ to His people! The breastplate appears to have been a sort of bag, in which Moses was commanded to deposit the Urim and Thummim (Ex. xxviii. 30; Lev. viii. 8). What these were cannot now be ascertained. The learned say, Urim means *lights*, and Thummim *truth*. More than this can probably never be known.

A plate of gold, on which was engraved, " Holiness to the Lord,' was attached to the turban of the high priest by a blue lace (Exodus xxviii. 36, 37).

Aaron and his posterity were chosen from among the Levites by Jehovah, to the sole exercise of the offices of the priesthood (Ex. xl. 12—15. Lev. viii. 6—9). Whoever else presumed to officiate, was punishable with death (Numb. iii. 10, 38, compared with xvi. 1—35 ; 2 Chron. xxvi. 16, 21).

The High Priest was the conductor of religious worship at the Tabernacle. His chief employment was to appease the wrath of God, under which the unbelief, and consequent disobedience of Israel was continually bringing them, and to secure His pardon and continued favour to the penitent nation, by offering the blood of atonement taken from the reconciling victims, brought for this purpose before the Altar, in the Court of the Tabernacle (Numb. xviii. 1 ; Heb. v. 1—4). In this work he was assisted by the common priests. Another part of his work was to see that the nation was kept well instructed in the divine law (Lev. x. 11 ; Neh. viii. 1—6 ;

Mal. ii. 7). In this also he was assisted by the common priests (Lev. x. 8—11), and by the Levites (Deut. xxxiii. 8—10; Neh. viii. 7,8), who were placed entirely at his command (Numb. iii. 5—7,9).

Things were so ordered, that upon the healthy state of the nation's piety, the very existence of this tribe was made to depend. The offerings on the altar or *table* (Mal. i. 7) of the Lord (Deut. xviii. 1—5; Numb. xviii. 8—21,24; 1 Cor. ix. 13, 14), were its only portion in Israel. If the national conscience was tender the offerings presented to the Lord flowed in freely, if the contrary, sparingly; and hence they became a test of the manner in which the people were instructed.

The priests were the only Levites permitted to officiate *in* the sacred dwelling or at the altar. Indeed, whilst the Tabernacle was occupied by the Divine Majesty, we consider that no other individual except Moses, Aaron and his sons, was permitted to approach nearer to it than the altar of the court. Death was the penalty incurred by any other who presumed to enter the sacred dwelling, or even to touch the altar (Numb. xviii. 1—7, 22). The work of presenting the national offerings to Jehovah belonged to the priesthood exclusively.

The work of packing the sacred furniture of the Tabernacle, preparatory to removal, was that of the high priest and common priests only (Numb. iv. 5—15). The work of carrying the various parts of the Tabernacle, was that of the common Levites, superintended by the priests. If, in carrying the sacred furniture the common Levite touched it, he was liable to suffer death (Numb. iv. 15; 2 Sam vi. 6, 7).

THE SACRIFICES AND OFFERINGS.

As a preface to further explanation of the Sacrifices, we may observe, that those, properly so called, were of three principal classes—the sin or trespass-offering, the whole burnt-offering, and the peace-offering. The animals offered—those bulls, goats, and lambs, whereby Christ was prefigured to the Jews, till He came as the innocent bearer of the wrath of Jehovah in place of the transgressors of His laws — were required to be free from "blemish," that is, without bodily imperfection.

The general rule with private individuals was to content themselves with bringing sin-offerings.

When national offerings for sin were presented, they were generally required to consist of all these classes.

Public and private members of the nation, also, sometimes voluntarily, and in case of some sins, by Divine appointment, approached God's altar with each class of offering. When this was the case, they were presented by the priest in the order mentioned above, that is, first, sin-offering; second, whole burnt-offering; third, peace-offering.

The blood of all these offerings atoned for sin; the peace-offering was, in addition, a feast of the Lord at His altar or *table* (Mal. i. 7), of which the Lord by the fire of His altar, the priest who offered it on behalf of the transgressor, and the sinner reconciled by it, partook. Hence the propriety of its being offered last.

We will now explain the offerings represented here. They consist entirely of the class called sin-offerings —

First. The Poor Man's Sin-offering.

If a man convinced of sin were so poor that he could not afford to present a lamb or kid to the Lord as a sin-offering, he was permitted to bring a turtle-dove or young pigeon (Lev. v. 7).

The group, picture 15, represents a poor family so engaged. The figures kneeling are the husband, wife, and child. Before

No. 15.

them stands the High Priest of the Lord. A common priest is in attendance. The head of the family is engaged in transferring the family's sins to the head of the dove, previously to consigning it to the priest to have its head wrung off, and its blood sprinkled on the side of the altar as an atonement.

If a man was too poor to offer so valuable a sacrifice as a dove, he was permitted to present a quantity of fleur instead (Lev. v. 11).

Second. The High Priest's Sin-of-ignorance Offering (Lev. iv. 1—12).

If a high priest sinned against the Lord through ignorance of the law, on making the discovery, he was required to atone for it. This he did with the blood of a bullock (Lev. iv. 3).

The picture, No. 16, p. 35, represents such a high priest transferring his sins to the bullock's head, preparatory to slaying it before the Lord (Lev. iv. 4). The attendant Levite is coaxing the animal to quietness.

This was one of the class of sin-offerings the blood of which required to be presented as an atonement in the Holy Place, by sprinkling seven times before the vail, and touching each horn of the altar of incense with it (see picture No. 11, page 27). The remainder of the blood was poured out by the sinning priest at the foot of the brazen altar in the court; and after placing some of the fatty parts of the sacrifice upon the altar, he sent the rest of the carcase outside the camp of Israel, there to be burnt (Lev. iv. 5—12). See the burning of this class of sin-offering represented in the picture of the encampment, No. 1, page 13, beyond the camp at the right, and in picture No. 18, page 38, in the foreground.

No. 16.

Third. The National Sin-of-ignorance Offering (Lev. iv. 13—21).

When the whole nation had sinned through ignorance of the law, on the discovery thereof, twelve of its elders, one from each tribe, were required to bring a bullock for a sin-offering, and to transfer to it the national sin by placing their hands on its head (Lev. iv. 15), preparatory to slaying it before the Lord.

The High Priest received the blood, proceeded with it to the Holy Place, sprinkled it seven times before the vail, and touched each horn of the altar of incense with it, so presenting the price of pardon and obtaining reconciliation for the sinning people. He then came out into the court, and after placing portions of the fat upon the altar, sent the whole carcase outside the camp by a "fit" man, there to be burnt (Lev. iv. 15—21).

So Jesus, "that He might sanctify the people with His own blood," suffered without the gate (Heb. xiii. 11, 12).

The picture (No. 17, p. 36) represents the High Priest, attended by a common priest, who carries a vessel in which to receive a portion of the blood, the bullock, and the elders in the act of confession and transference.

The High Priest's and the Nation's Sin-offerings, the blood of which was presented to the Lord within the Tabernacle, appear to have been the only ones burnt outside the camp. The Sin-offerings of private individuals became the property of the priest, who presented their blood to the Lord on the altar of the court, with the exception of the fatty parts consumed thereon, and was required to be eaten in the court of the Tabernacle by the priests only (Lev. vi. 24—30, compared with x. 16—18).

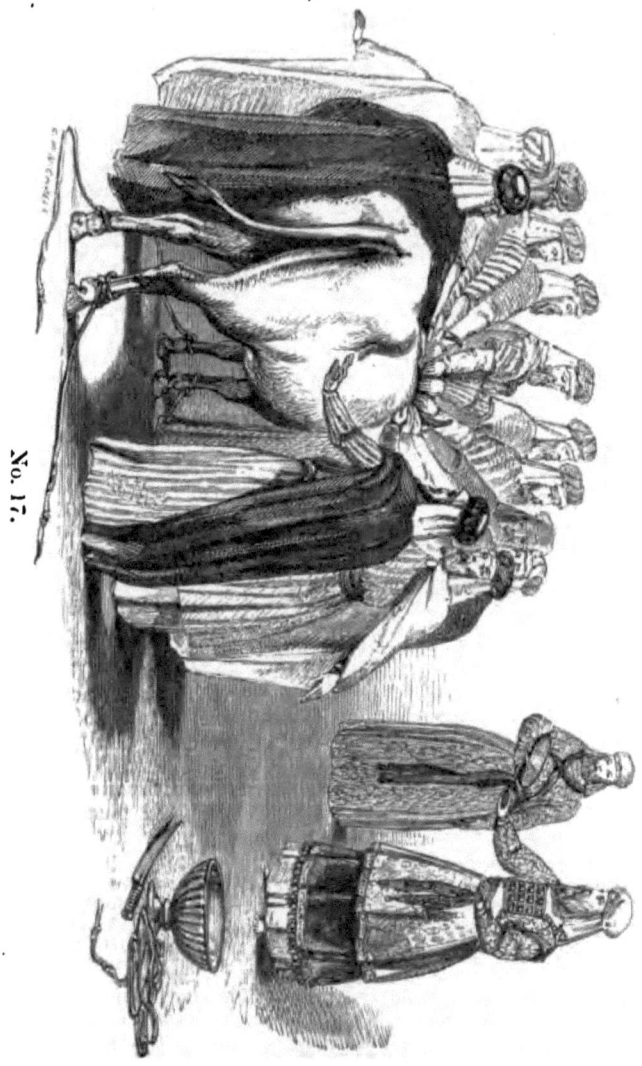

No. 17.

Fourth. The Great Day of Atonement Sin-offerings (Lev. xvi.).
These were presented once a year. On this day, the nation assembled around the Tabernacle, and "afflicted" itself the whole day for its sins (Lev. xvi. 29).

The High Priest put off his glorious robes in the Holy Place (ver. 4, 23, 24), washed himself, and came out into the court attired like a

No. 18

common priest (ver. 4). Before the altar stood a bullock, for his sin-offering (ver. 3). The High Priest first transferred his own sins to his sin-offering bullock by placing his hands on its head (picture No. 16, page 35, may be supposed to represent him so engaged) ; he then slew it, and carried some of its blood into the Most Holy Place. In the picture of the Ark (page 28), he is seen sprinkling a few drops with his finger on the Mercy-seat, and seven times before it. He thus atoned for his own sins (ver. 14).

He now took one of the nation's sin-offerings, which on this occasion consisted of two young goats (picture 19).

On the head of one of these he laid the people's sins, by placing his hands thereon ; then slew it, received its blood, returned with it to the Most Holy Place, sprinkled a few drops on the Mercy-seat, and seven times before the Mercy-seat (ver. 15). He again returned to the court, and the other, the scape-goat, was brought before him (ver. 7—10). He transferred the national guilt to its head, by laying both his hands thereon, at the same time confessing " over him all the iniquities of the children of Israel, and all their transgressions in all their sins, putting them upon the head of the goat" (ver. 21). Thus laden, he sent him out of the camp alive by the hand of a "fit" man to be set free in the wilderness.

No. 19.

The sacred text explains the meaning of these symbolic actions in the following words : " And the goat shall bear upon him all their iniquities into a land not inhabited : and he shall let the goat go into the wilderness " (ver. 22).

May Christ enable each of us to cast our burden of sins on Him by faith, so that we may find Him to be to us all that this scape-goat was intended to represent to Israel ; for " surely He hath borne our griefs and carried our sorrows," and " the Lord hath laid upon Him the iniquity of us all " (Isa. liii. 4, 6).

The High Priest then returned to the Holy Place, cast off his garments, washed his flesh with water, and put on his glorious robes (Lev. xvi. 24). Then he came to the brazen altar, and offered two rams, for his own and the people's whole burnt-offering (ver. 24, 3, 5) ; presented some of the fatty parts of the slain sin-offerings on the altar, and sent the rest outside the camp, where they were wholly burnt (ver. 25, 27).

The man who conducted the scape-goat out of the camp into the wilderness, and the men who dragged out the sin-offerings of the priest and people, were all required to wash their clothes and bathe their flesh in water, before returning to the camp, now made clean by the blood of atonement (ver. 26—28).

Doubtless these ceremonial purifications suggested to the pious the use of such expressions as these—" Wash me throughly from mine iniquity, and cleanse me from my sin " (Ps. li. 2). " Unto Him that loved us, and washed us from our sins in His own blood" Rev. i. 5).

The rites of the Great Day of Atonement having now all been performed, according to the requirements of the divine law, the High Priest very-probably went up to the altar of burnt-offering and, turning his back to it and his face to the people assembled at its foot, with uplifted hands, pronounced in the name of the Lord, and in the hearing of at least its twelve representative princes, the prescribed form of national blessing --

No. 20.

"The Lord bless thee, and keep thee : the Lord make His face shine upon thee, and be gracious unto thee : the Lord lift up His countenance upon thee, and give thee peace" (Numb. vi. 22—26). And then he dismissed the assembled nation to their tents in "peace" with God.

LORD JESUS, THIS PEACE GIVE UNTO US.

The reader is recommended to peruse the Epistle to the Hebrews as being the Divine interpretation of the Mosaic Economy.